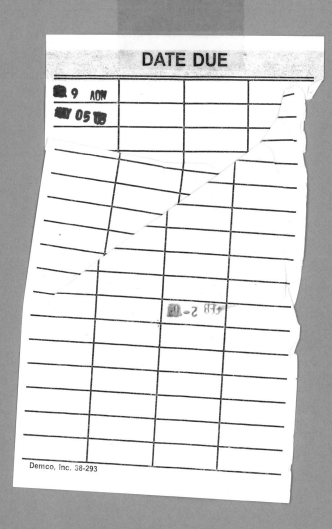

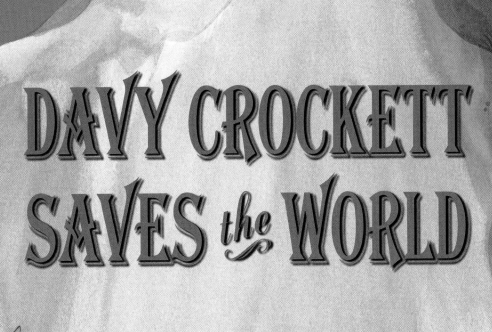

DAVY CROCKETT SAVES the WORLD

BY ROSALYN SCHANZER

HarperCollins Publishers

For Steve

Davy Crockett Saves the World
Copyright © 2001 by Rosalyn Schanzer
Printed in U.S.A.
All rights reserved.
www.harperchildrens.com
Library of Congress Cataloging-in-Publication Data
Schanzer, Rosalyn.
Davy Crockett saves the world / by Rosalyn Schanzer.—1st ed.
p.   cm.
Summary: Davy Crockett stops the evil Halley's Comet from destroying the world,
and wins the heart of Sally Sugartree in the process.
ISBN 0-688-16991-0 — ISBN 0-688-16992-9 (lib. bdg.)
1. Crockett, Davy, 1786–1836—Juvenile fiction.   [1. Crockett, Davy, 1786–1836—
Fiction.   2. Tall tales.]   I. Title.
PZ7.S3339 Dav   2001   00-32021
[Fic]—dc21   CIP
AC
2 3 4 5 6 7 8 9 10
❖

AUTHOR'S NOTE

The real Davy Crockett (1786–1836) was a famous frontiersman, hunter, scout, and quick-witted storyteller from Tennessee who became a member of Congress and died defending the Alamo. So thoroughly did he capture the public imagination that, between 1835 and 1855, a series of comic almanacs rigged to look like they were written by Crockett himself became big best-sellers. Sandwiched between information about stars, tides, and the weather were outrageous drawings and tall tales about Davy Crockett that didn't give a hoot about the facts. The story in this book was written in the spirit of these almanacs and sometimes even stirs together a concoction of events and phrases found therein.

I reckon by now you've heard of Davy Crockett, the greatest woodsman who ever lived. Why, Davy could whip ten times his weight in wildcats and drink the Mississippi River dry. He combed his hair with a rake, shaved his beard with an ax, and could run so fast that, whenever he

went out, the trees had to step aside to keep from getting knocked down.

Folks always crow about the deeds of Davy Crockett, but the biggest thing he ever did was to save the world. This here story tells exactly how he did it, and every single word is true, unless it is false.

About the time our tale begins, the world was in a heap of trouble. A way past the clouds and far beyond all the stars and planets in outer space, scientists with telescopes had discovered the biggest, baddest ball of fire and ice and brimstone ever to light up the heavens.

Its name was Halley's Comet, and it was hurling itself lickety-split straight toward America. Why, its tail alone was two million miles long. If it were to hit the earth, everyone would be blown to smithereens!

The President of the United States started getting big piles of letters telling him to stop Halley's Comet before it was too late. He made a law telling the comet it couldn't crash into the earth, but the comet paid no attention. It just kept speeding toward America and growing bigger every day.

Finally the President had an idea. He had heard of a brave man named Davy Crockett, who lived somewhere in the mountains far away. He put an advertisement in all the newspapers in America that said:

<u>WANTED BY THE PRESIDENT</u>
<u>OF THE UNITED STATES</u>
DAVY CROCKETT
TO PULL THE TAIL OFF OF
HALLEY'S COMET

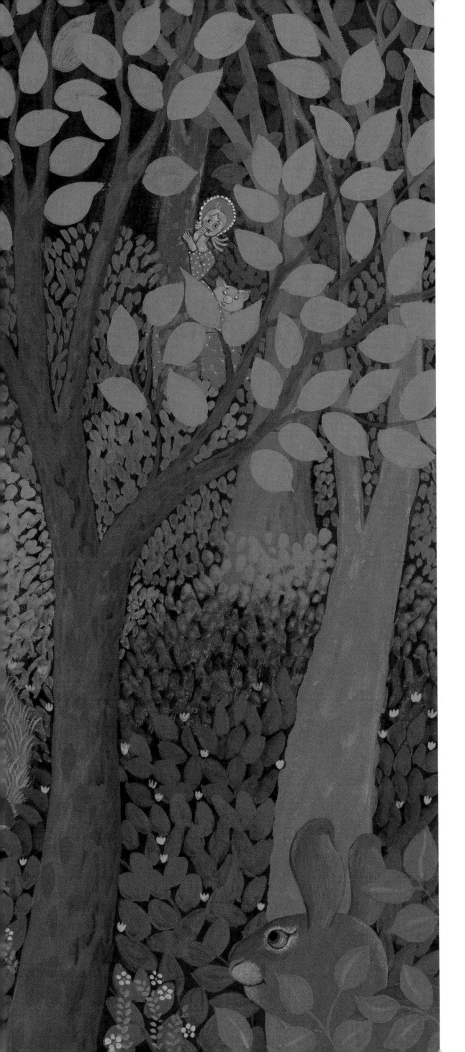

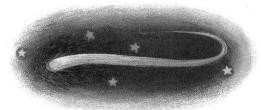

Meanwhile, Davy Crockett didn't know a thing about any comet. He had no idea that the earth was even in danger. Davy was off in the forest with his pet bear, Death Hug. He was teaching himself to dance so that he could impress a real purty gal named Sally Sugartree, who could dance a hole through a double oak floor. He was not reading any newspapers.

It took two whole weeks, but once Davy had learned all the latest dances, he combed his hair nice and slow with his rake, shaved his face real careful-like with his ax, and sauntered off toward Sally Sugartree's cabin just as easy as you please.

All this time, of course, Halley's Comet was getting closer and closer to the earth and moving faster by the minute.

Now, Sally Sugartree was not just purty, but she was right smart too. Sally read the newspaper front to back every day, and she knew all about Halley's Comet. She had also seen the advertisement from the President.

Sally climbed up a fifty-foot hickory tree and commenced to look for Davy Crockett. Before long, she spotted him a way far off in the forest. Sally grabbed up her newspaper and waved it around just as hard as she could. When Davy saw her, he grinned and started to walk a mite faster.

As soon as Davy got close enough, Sally jumped right out of that tree. Davy caught her in his arms and gave her such a hug that her tongue stuck out half a foot and her eyes popped out like a lobster's. Then she showed Davy the want ad from the President.

Davy still didn't know what Halley's Comet was, but if the President of the United States wanted to see him, he would waste no time getting to Washington. He bridled up Death Hug and set out like a high-powered hurrycane. He could dance with Sally later.

Death Hug ran so fast that rocks and trees and cows and snakes and other varmints all flew out behind him.

By the time they reached the White House, Halley's Comet was getting so close that there wasn't a minute to lose.

The President told Davy to climb the highest mountain he could find right away, and to wring that comet's tail off before it could destroy the earth. Then the President posed with Davy for pictures and pretended to look calm.

Davy combed his hair with his rake, rolled up his sleeves, and ate a big plateful of pickled rattlesnake brains fried by lightning to give him energy. Then he commenced to climb all the way to the top of Eagle Eye Peak in the Great Smoky Mountains.

Eagle Eye Peak was so high you could see every state and river and mountain in a whole geography book.

You could also look a way far off into outer space. By the time Davy reached the top, it was night.

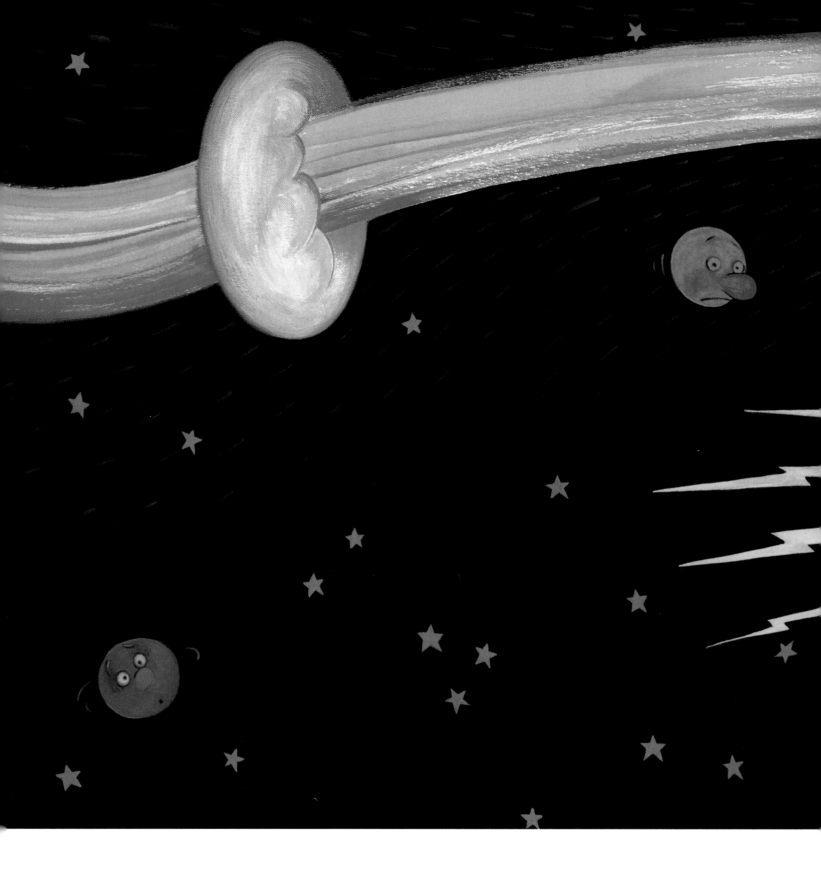

Halley's Comet spotted Davy Crockett right away. It took a flying leap and zoomed past all the stars and planets. Then it laughed and headed straight toward Davy like a red-hot cannonball!

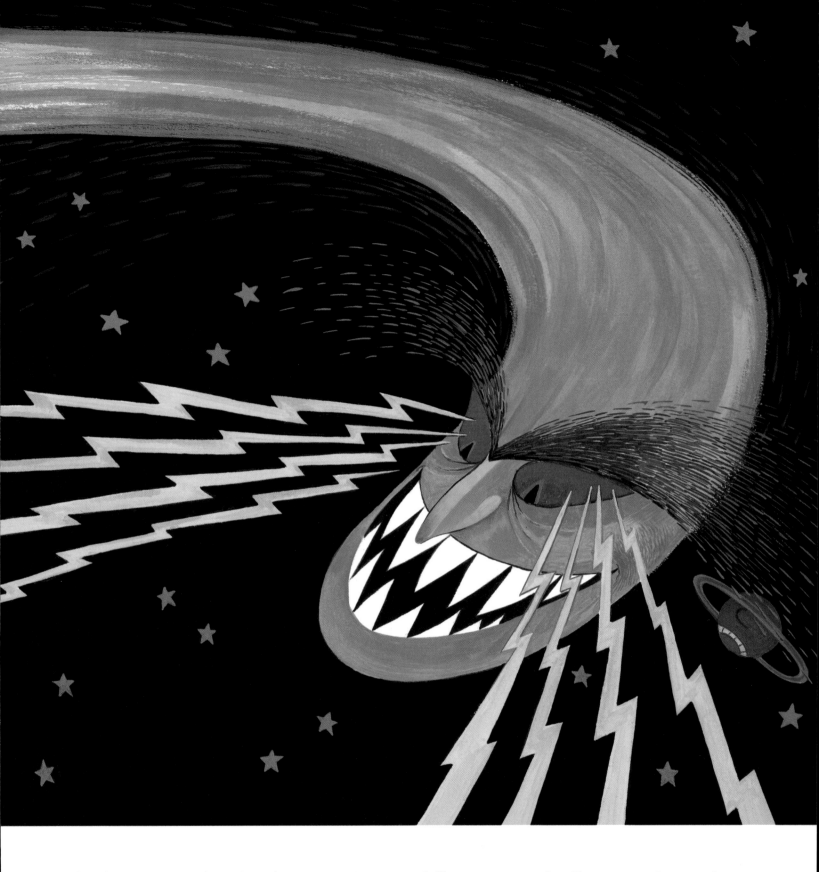

Lightning and thunder shot out of its eyes! So many sparks flew out of its tail that, even though it was night, the entire countryside lit up and all the roosters set to crowin'!

That comet must have thought Davy looked mighty tender, for it licked its chops, howled louder than a hundred tornadoes, and roared toward him with its mouth wide open!

This made Davy so mad that he jumped right over its shoulders and onto its back. Then he planted his teeth around the comet's neck and hung on. Halley's Comet spun around and around like a whirlwind trying to throw Davy off, but it couldn't.

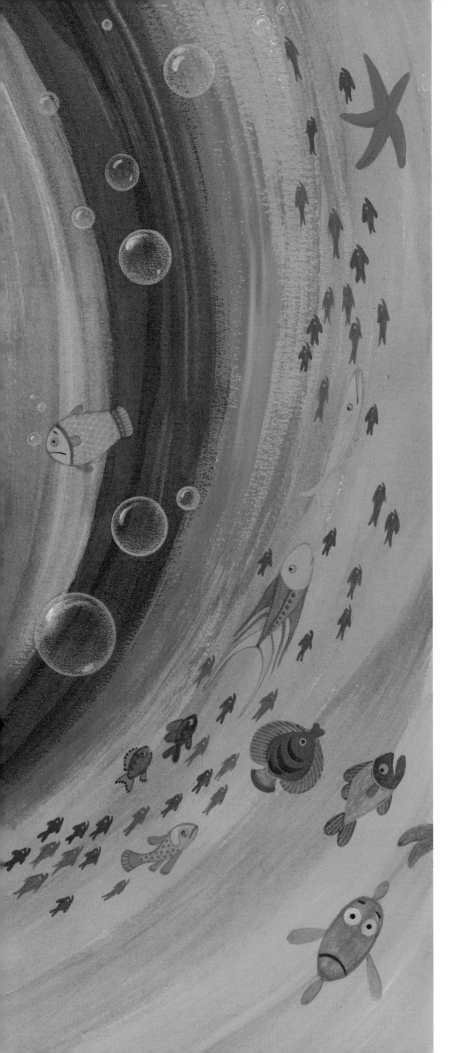

Next off, that comet tried to drown Davy by diving into the Atlantic Ocean. The water got so all-fired hot that it boiled! The whole world was covered with steam, and the sun didn't shine as bright as usual for a month.

Just in time, the ocean put out that comet's fire and melted all its ice. It washed up on an island, and before it could grow back to its original size, Davy grabbed what was left of Halley's tail, spun around seventeen times, and hurled the comet back into outer space. It was so discombobulated that the next time it ever came in this direction, it missed the earth by 39 million miles.

That's how Davy Crockett saved the world. In fact, he did such a good job that there was a huge parade in his honor, he got to marry Sally Sugartree, and he was even elected to Congress.

Of course, that infernal fireball singed the hair right off Davy's head. A whole new crop grew back in tufts like grass and kept in such a snarl that he couldn't even comb it without breaking his rake.

That's why these days Davy Crockett always wears a coonskin cap.